THE THREE LITTLE FISH

AND THE

FOR MARTHA — K.G.

FOR MY FISHY IVY,
WHO MAKES HER HOUSE OUT OF FABRIC,
FOR MY FISHY RALEIGH,
WHO MAKES HIS HOUSE OUT OF SKATEBOARDS,
AND FOR MY FISHY RUSSELL,
WHO MAKES HIS HOUSE OUT OF MAGIC!
— J.G.

ISBN-13: 978-0-439-71963-6
ISBN-10: 0-439-71963-1

11 10 9 8 7 6 5 4 3 2 1 09 10 11 12 13

Printed in the U.S.A.
This edition first printing, January 2009

BY KEN GEIST

ILLUSTRATED BY JULIA GORTON

Cartwheel
·B·O·O·K·S·®

SCHOLASTIC INC.
NEW YORK TORONTO LONDON AUCKLAND SYDNEY
MEXICO CITY NEW DELHI HONG KONG BUENOS AIRES

Once upon a time, there lived a mama fish and her three little fish, Jim, Tim, and Kim. "It is now time," said the mama, "for each of you to make a home in the deep blue sea." So off they went.

THE FIRST LITTLE FISH, NAMED JIM, SWAM AWAY AND MET A SEA HORSE PLAYING IN SOME SEAWEED.

"CAN I HAVE SOME OF THE SEAWEED SO I CAN BUILD A HOUSE?"

"TAKE AS MUCH AS YOU CAN CARRY," SAID THE SEA HORSE.

JIM GATHERED THE SEAWEED AND MADE A WEEDY LITTLE HOUSE.

JIM HAD JUST FINISHED BUILDING HIS SEAWEED HOUSE WHEN HE HEARD THE BIG BAD SHARK KNOCKING AT THE DOOR.

"LITTLE FISH, LITTLE FISH, LET ME COME IN."

THE LITTLE FISH TREMBLED AND REPLIED,

"NOT BY THE SKIN OF MY FINNY FIN FIN!"

"THEN I'LL MUNCH AND I'LL CRUNCH AND I'LL SMASH YOUR HOUSE IN,"

ROARED THE SHARK.

SO THE BIG BAD SHARK
MUNCHED AND HE CRUNCHED
AND HE ATE UP EVERY BIT
OF THE SEAWEED HOUSE.

AND JIM SWAM AWAY—JUST IN TIME.

SOON JIM FOUND HIS BROTHER. TIM SAID,

"DON'T WORRY, JIM. WE FISH STICK TOGETHER!

YOU CAN HELP ME BUILD A SANDY LITTLE HOUSE."

Jim and Tim had just started to relax in the sandy little house when the Big Bad Shark came knocking at the door.

"Little fish, little fish, let me come in."

TO WHICH THE BRAVE LITTLE FISH REPLIED,

"NOT BY THE SKIN OF MY FINNY FIN FIN!"

"THEN I'LL MUNCH AND I'LL CRUNCH AND I'LL SMASH YOUR HOUSE IN," ROARED THE SHARK.

SO THE BIG BAD SHARK MUNCHED AND HE CRUNCHED UNTIL HE GOT A SANDY MOUTHFUL AND THE HOUSE CRUMBLED.

JIM AND TIM SWAM AND SWAM...

. . . UNTIL THEY REACHED THEIR SISTER, KIM.
KIM WAS SETTING UP HER HOUSE
IN AN OLD WOODEN SHIP.

"THE BIG BAD SHARK DESTROYED OUR HOUSES."

"DON'T WORRY. YOU CAN LIVE WITH ME," SAID KIM. AND THEY DID.

THE THREE LITTLE FISH HAD JUST FINISHED LUNCH WHEN THEY HEARD THE BIG BAD SHARK KNOCKING AT THEIR DOOR.

"LITTLE FISH, LITTLE FISH, LET ME COME IN."

TO WHICH THE SMART FISH REPLIED,

"NOT BY THE SKIN OF MY FINNY FIN FIN!"

"THEN I'LL MUNCH AND I'LL CRUNCH AND I'LL SMASH YOUR HOUSE IN," ROARED THE SHARK.

THE BIG BAD SHARK MUNCHED AND HE CRUNCHED BUT HE COULD NOT SMASH THE HOUSE IN...

AND
ALL HIS TEETH
FELL OUT!

THE THREE LITTLE FISH WERE SAFE AT LAST.